The Odyssey

Diane Redmond

Illustrated by Barry Smith

A & C BLACK • LONDON

Contents

A Letter from the Playwright

To open the treasures of the Greek Myths to children is a joy and a privilege. There is beauty, adventure, wonder and terror in the story of *The Odyssey*, plus the magic of gods, monsters and heroes. But, it is complicated! I always start by telling the story of *The Odyssey*. It's utterly spell-binding and has enough tension in it to keep even the noisiest children rapt. Begin where Homer began, with the Fall of Troy. Brave Odysseus, the conquering hero, is all set to go home to Ithaca after ten long years of war against the Trojans. But he hasn't reckoned with the Gods on Mount Olympus. Poseidon, God of the Sea and brother of Zeus, is furious with Odysseus for destroying his favourite city, Troy. In a filthy temper he churns up the oceans and sends Odysseus and the last of the mighty Greek army spinning around the world where they meet monsters, demons, devils and witches. Luckily for Odysseus they also meet Athene, Goddess of Wisdom and Zeus' favourite daughter. She and Hermes, the winged Messenger of the Gods, protect Odysseus and after ten more years of blood-curdling adventures Odysseus returns home to Ithaca where his wife, Penelope, and his son, Telemachus, have prayed daily for his return. But even when he's home Odysseus has troubles.

His son has grown into a man and doesn't recognise him and his palace is full of noisy, drunken strangers who have been trying to marry HIS wife. Determined to prove himself, Odysseus challenges the men to bend his golden bow. Penelope knows that only her husband can bend the bow and as she watches the stranger bend it and shoot her enemies, Penelope realises that AT LAST her husband, Odysseus, King of Ithaca, has come home!

It is a play of extremes and cannot be compromised into something comfortable. Let the children go big time into the experience, they'll rarely get the opportunity of playing so many monsters in their life! As they work their way through the play, I hope they'll begin to see the highs and the lows of the story. There are scenes where they'll shout and scream and others where they'll need to be still and thoughtful. Sometimes they'll make the audience laugh and other times they might make them weep. That's the joy of acting and the wonder of the theatre, something that's not changed a jot since Homer wrote *The Odyssey* three thousand years ago.

The Gods go with you!

Characters In Order Of Appearance

The Crew: 1 Odysseus
            2 Polites
            3 Elpenor
            4 Eurylochus
            5 Stavros
            6 Mikos
            7 Mentor
            8 Castor
            (and as many more
            as you wish, placed
            down the centre of
            the boat formation)

The Greek Chorus

The Gods: Poseidon, the Sea God
            Hermes, messenger of the Gods
            Zeus, God of Gods
            Athene, Goddess of Wisdom

Polyphemus the Cyclops
Circe the Witch
Scylla the Six-headed Monster
Tiresias
Telemachus
The Suitors: Polybus the Cretan
               Alexander the Spartan
Penelope, Odysseus' wife

List of Scenes and their Locations

Act 1
Scene 1 – The End of the Trojan War   : On Land
Scene 2 – Meeting One-Eye   : The Cyclops' Island
Scene 3 – Circe the Witch   : Circe's Island

[Interval if desired]

Act 2

Scene 1 – Three More Monsters   : On the Sea
Scene 2 – Apollo's Sacred Bull   : Apollo's Island
Scene 3 – The Shadows of the Dead   : In Hades
Scene 4 – The Bending of the Bow   : Ithaca

The playing time is approximately 50 minutes without an interval.

Act 1, Scene 1 – The End of the Trojan War

On Land. The GODS, ATHENE, POSEIDON AND HERMES, are seated on Olympus, stage right. The CREW and the CHORUS swagger on from the other side of the stage. They cheer and wave their arms until they reach centre-stage where they stop.

CREW AND
CHORUS:
Hurray! Hurray!
We beat the Trojans!
We won the war!

(ODYSSEUS, their leader, enters.)

CREW AND
CHORUS:
(chanting in unison)
We fight with Odysseus, we're his men.
We conquered Troy – and we'll do it again!
We fight and we fight – we <u>never</u> give up.
Greeks don't go in for that kinda stuff!

(ODYSSEUS holds up his hand, commanding their instant silence.)

ODYSSEUS:
The Trojan War is over – long live the Greeks!

CREW AND
CHORUS:
Yeaahh!

ODYSSEUS:
Ten years we've been fighting this war – <u>ten years</u>!
But we won – <u>we won</u>!

ELPENOR:
Now we can go home, my Lord. Home to Ithaca.

ODYSSEUS:
(sighing) Yes Elpenor, home... back to my wife, Penelope, and my baby boy.

STAVROS:
Baby boy! Not any more, my Lord. We left Ithaca ten years ago. Your son will be <u>ten</u> by now!

ODYSSEUS:
My son, ten years old! Oh, I can't wait to see him.
To the boat, to the boat. We're going home!

CREW AND CHORUS:	Yeaahh! We're going home!

(The CHORUS split off from the CREW and take up their positions stage left. The CREW sit down centre-stage in the shape of a boat and pretend to row in unison. Three of the CHORUS speak the following lines.)

VOICE ONE:	You'd think that after ten years of fighting Odysseus would deserve to go home. But Poseidon the Sea God doesn't think so.
VOICE TWO:	Odysseus and his army have just destroyed Troy – Poseidon's favourite city – and he's <u>furious</u>!
VOICE THREE:	Let me tell you something about the Gods. They all live on Mount Olympus, over there... *(All the members of the CHORUS point towards OLYMPUS where the GODS are seated, except for ZEUS who is standing.)* Zeus is the God of Gods, the most powerful. His brother Poseidon is the Sea God, and Athene, Zeus' favourite daughter, is the Goddess of Wisdom. The little one is Hermes, Messenger of the Gods.

(There is a sound of clashing cymbals. On Olympus POSEIDON and HERMES stand up.)

POSEIDON:	*(pointing, with his trident, to the other side of the stage)* Look at Troy! Look what the Greeks have done to <u>my</u> holy city.
HERMES:	All's fair in love and war, so they say.
POSEIDON:	<u>Fair</u>! You call the destruction of Troy fair?
HERMES:	The Trojans have been fighting too, you know. They've been killing and torturing the Greeks for ten years now.
POSEIDON:	*(shaking his trident)* Grrrr! Odysseus has destroyed my city. He won't get away with it. I will have <u>VENGEANCE</u>!

(ZEUS enters stage right. He strides to Olympus. ATHENE, holding her silver spear, rises to her feet.)

ZEUS: Wait, Poseidon. Still your oceans.

ATHENE: Odysseus is under <u>my</u> protection.

POSEIDON: W-H-A-T?

ATHENE: His wife, Penelope, prays to me every day for the safe return of her husband. I intend to save Odysseus.

POSEIDON: You! Get out of my way.

ZEUS: Careful, brother. Athene is my daughter.

ATHENE: *(proud and powerful)* I am the Goddess of Wisdom.

POSEIDON: *(menacingly)* I am the God of the Sea and the Winds. I will <u>destroy</u> Odysseus.

ATHENE: I challenge you to a contest, Poseidon. My wisdom versus your strength.

POSEIDON: <u>Wisdom</u>! Don't make me laugh. *(He points to the middle of the stage, where ODYSSEUS and his CREW are rowing in slow, gentle motion.)* Look where your mortal fool's going now. Due south, straight to the Island of the Cyclops. My son Polyphemus will give the Greeks a warm welcome. Ha... Ha... Ha!

(POSEIDON exits stage right. ATHENE, ZEUS and HERMES sit down quietly, in their positions on Olympus. Most of the CHORUS make the sound of a storm, blowing and whistling like the wind. Three of the CHORUS speak the following lines.)

VOICE ONE: Poseidon stirred up the seas of the world.

(The sound of the storm gets louder and stronger. The CREW row faster and harder.)

VOICE TWO:	He blew Odysseus and his men across the sea to the Island of the Cyclops, the hideous, one-eyed monster who eats men – <u>alive</u>!
VOICE THREE:	Poseidon's son is a cyclops – Polyphemus! Last week he ate forty-two sailors, two dolphins and a mermaid!

(The storm blows itself out as the CHORUS reduce their storm effects and the CREW row more slowly as the noises gently die away.)

Act 1, Scene 2 – Meeting One-Eye

The Cyclops' Island. ODYSSEUS and the CREW stop rowing. They remain seated as they look curiously about.

ELPENOR:	Great Gods, where are we?
STAVROS:	I dunno but that was some storm that blew us. North, east, south, west –
EURYLOCHUS:	Oh, don't remind me... *(He retches.)*

(CASTOR backs away from EURYLOCHUS.)

CASTOR:	<u>Ugh</u>! That's disgusting, Eurylochus!
EURYLOCHUS:	I can't help it. I'm sick of the sea, Castor. I've been tossed back and forth across the blooming Mediterranean for <u>ten years</u>!
STAVROS:	I thought we were going home.
ELPENOR:	Stop arguing, all of you! Come on, we'll search the island.

(The CREW stand up and exit, leaving ODYSSEUS alone. There is the sound of chimes. ATHENE leaves Olympus and walks across to the middle of the stage to stand before ODYSSEUS.)

ATHENE:	*(saluting with her spear)* Beware, Odysseus. Beware!
ODYSSEUS:	Athene! Goddess of Wisdom, I salute you.

ATHENE: Poseidon, the Sea God is angry with you.

ODYSSEUS: Angry with me? Why?

ATHENE: Because you destroyed his holy city, Troy. You burnt it to the ground.

ODYSSEUS: I'm a warrior, Goddess. It's my job to fight.

ATHENE: You will die unless you can outwit the Sea God.

ODYSSEUS: *(astonished)* I have no skills to fight Poseidon.
Oh, help me, Goddess. Please?

ATHENE: I will protect you, Odysseus, but you must use your cunning. Think... think... think...

(The wind chimes sound as ATHENE returns to her position on Olympus. The CREW enter and find ODYSSEUS rooted to the spot, staring into space.)

ELPENOR: *(shaking ODYSSEUS by the arm)* My Lord! Are you ill?

ODYSSEUS: *(thoughtfully)* No, no... I'm just thinking.

EURYLOCHUS: *(interrupting)* I'm ill – I'm starving!

MIKOS: You're always hungry.

EURYLOCHUS: I'm always hungry, Mikos, 'cause we never eat!

(We hear bleating noises. These are made by the CHORUS. The noise continues for some time.)

MENTOR: Sheep!

EURYLOCHUS: *(walking towards the bleating noise)* Sheep! Yummee – supper!

ODYSSEUS: No, Eurylochus! Don't touch those sheep.
(He turns to the CREW.) Follow me...

(ODYSSEUS leads his CREW off stage left, to the front of the CHORUS and then behind them. As they re-enter from the back of the stage the CHORUS stop bleating. The CREW gaze around, clearly overawed.)

CASTOR: Blimey! Where are we now?

ELPENOR: An enormous cave...

MENTOR: Who can live here?

POLITES: Maybe a shepherd. Look! Here's some cheese... and milk... *(He mimes picking up a piece of cheese and drinking from a bowl of milk.)*

EURYLOCHUS: Cheese and milk – forget it! I want <u>meat</u>.

(The CHORUS start to make bleating noises, sending EURYLOCHUS into a frenzy.)

EURYLOCHUS: Grrrr! I need <u>meat</u>!

(POLITES grabs EURYLOCHUS by the arm.)

POLITES: Eurylochus! We must wait for the shepherd to return. Maybe he'll offer us some food.

EURYLOCHUS: *(sulkily)* Oh... he could be hours!

(EURYLOCHUS and the crew slump wearily to the ground.)

ODYSSEUS: Cheer up, look what I've got here. *(He takes a bottle from his tunic and hands it to EURYLOCHUS.)* Nectar, the wine of the Gods.

EURYLOCHUS: Oooh, thank you. *(He raises bottle to his lips.)*

ODYSSEUS: Stop! Just a sip! It'll blow your head off.

(EURYLOCHUS sips from the bottle.)

EURYLOCHUS: Nectar. *(He rolls his eyes.)* Mmm... Here, Stavros.

(EURYLOCHUS passes the bottle to STAVROS who takes a sip and smacks his lips.)

STAVROS: Mmmmm, brilliant!

(MIKOS stands and drinks, then drinks again and starts to sway drunkenly. There is a loud rumbling noise from off stage. MIKOS freezes in surprise.)

MIKOS: What's that?

(The rumbling continues from off stage.)

POLITES: It's an earthquake!

MENTOR: It's a volcano!

(The CYCLOPS thunders on stage left.)

ALL: Great balls of fire! It's a cyclops!

(CREW hide behind ODYSSEUS who shrinks from the CYCLOPS' hands.)

CYCLOPS: Graagh! Graaaagh! What's this? Strangers, in my cave?
                       *(CYCLOPS slams an enormous boulder over the cave
                       entrance, or mimes the action.)* Graaagh! Where are you?

(ODYSSEUS boldly steps forwards. CREW gape in horror.)

ODYSSEUS: Sir!

CYCLOPS: Huh? Who is it that calls me sir?

ODYSSEUS: *(boldly)* Strangers who are lost and tired.

CYCLOPS: Oooh! Strangers eh? Yum yum! *(He lumbers towards
                       ODYSSEUS.)*

POLITES: Odysseus! Watch out – he'll eat you!

ODYSSEUS: *(dodging the CYCLOPS)* Sir, forgive our intrusion.

CYCLOPS: <u>Our</u>? Mmmmmm... more than one. Which of you to eat first? *(The CREW huddle in a terrified group, trembling with fear.)*

EURYLOCHUS: *(beseechingly)* My Lord, I beg you, <u>get away</u>!

(ODYSSEUS ignores his pleas. He grabs the bottle from MIKOS and swaggers over to the CYCLOPS, holding it out.)

ODYSSEUS: Great God, may I offer you some sweet, mellow wine...?

STAVROS: (aside) That stuff'll knock him sideways.

(CYCLOPS opens the bottle and peers inside it with his one eye. He grunts happily.)

CYCLOPS: Wine, eh? Very nice. Glug... glug... glug... glug! *(tipsily)* 'Ere, what's your name, stranger?

ODYSSEUS: *(taken by surprise)* My name! Er, my name, Great God, is <u>Nobody</u>.

CYCLOPS: *(silly and giggly from the wine)* Mr Nobody! *(He yawns.)* Awww... I'm so sleepy... *(He falls asleep.)* Z z z z...

(ODYSSEUS springs to his feet in a flash.)

ODYSSEUS: Quick – Stavros, Mikos, Castor – grab that stick! *(He shouts impatiently at his CREW who stare at him, bemused.)* <u>Move</u>! Quickly! Before he wakes up.

(The CREW grab a stick from the ground.)

ODYSSEUS: Right – shove it in the fire. Turn it... turn it. Go on, keep turning!

(The CREW mime turning the stick in a fire. The CYCLOPS stirs and grunts then crawls drunkenly off stage.)

ODYSSEUS: *(looking at the stick)* That'll do. Pull it out of the fire. <u>Quickly</u>!

(The CREW mime the action of pulling the stick out of the fire.)

STAVROS: What're we gonna do with it?

ODYSSEUS: Shove it in his eye!

(The CREW stop and stare at Odysseus in horror. From off stage we hear the sound of the CYCLOPS' loud snores.)

ODYSSEUS: <u>Move</u>! Before he wakes up.

MIKOS: Eye eye, sir!

(MIKOS, STAVROS and CASTOR move to the side of the stage where the CYCLOPS snores in the wings.)

ODYSSEUS: On the count of three, shove it in his eye.

(The CREW grimace but point the stick towards the wings.)

CREW: One... two... three!

CREW AND
CHORUS: *(together)* Aaaaaaaaaghhhhh!

(The CREW hold the stick and shove the end of it off stage.)

VOICE ONE: Stavros, Mikos and Castor charged at the sleeping Cyclops and shoved the red hot stick in his single eye! Ugh!

(The CHORUS make faces.)

CHORUS: Eeergh!

CYCLOPS: *(from off stage)* Aaaaaghhhh!

VOICE TWO: They turned and turned the stick until it was too slimy to turn any more!

CYCLOPS: *(calls from off stage)* My eye! My eye!

VOICE THREE: Slowly they backed away from the screaming Cyclops and waited...

(There is a tense pause. The CREW slowly pull the stick away from the wings. The CYCLOPS comes back on stage, having broken the tissue paper eye of his costume, while off stage.)

CYCLOPS: Ahhhhhhhh! *(He reaches out blindly.)* I'll get you, Nobody! I'll get you!

STAVROS: Oh yeah? You'll have to catch us first, One-Eye.

ODYSSEUS: Shut up, Stavros. We've got to get out of here!

(ODYSSEUS and the CREW look around for a way out of the cave.)

VOICE ONE: Odysseus and his men were trapped in the cave!

VOICE TWO: They couldn't shift the huge boulder that blocked the entrance.

VOICE THREE: Nobody could but the Cyclops himself.

(The CYCLOPS lumbers. The CREW scatter in terror.)

CHORUS: Baaaaa... Baaaaaaa...!

(ODYSSEUS stops dead in his tracks.)

ODYSSEUS: *(smiling)* I've got it!

(The other members of the CHORUS continue to bleat quietly as VOICE ONE speaks.)

VOICE ONE: Cunning Odysseus had a brainwave. He told his men to disguise themselves as sheep.

(ODYSSEUS dashes to a corner of the stage and throws sheepskins to the CREW. The CREW throw them over their shoulders. They head towards the boulder blocking the entrance. The CYCLOPS stops to listen to his sheep.)

ODYSSEUS: *(addressing the CREW)* Bleat for your lives! *(very loudly)*
                  Baaaa... Baaaa...

CYCLOPS: Ahhhhh... my little ones. *(He moves the big boulder.)*
                  Out you go. Boo-hooo-hooo!

(The CYCLOPS tenderly pats each 'sheep' as they skip by. The CREW exit and run around the back of the CHORUS. They re-enter and stand in front of the stage to taunt the CYCLOPS.)

CREW: *(jubilant)* Yeee-haw!

CYCLOPS: *(peering in the direction of the shouting)* Huh? Whassat?

ODYSSEUS: Me, One-Eye! Your bleating breakfast! Baaaa!

CYCLOPS: You tricked me, Nobody!

ODYSSEUS: *(wildly)* Yes, I tricked you.

CYCLOPS: How dare you? I am Poseidon's son!

ELPENOR: Oh, no. Not Poseidon's son!

POLITES: Now we're really in trouble!

EURYLOCHUS: Let's get out of here!

(ODYSSEUS and CREW sit down quickly in the shape of a boat and begin to row.)

CYCLOPS: *(raging)* Poseidon! Father, revenge me! Revenge me!

(The CYCLOPS exits stage left. The CREW mime rowing then slow down gradually and freeze into stillness. Lights down.)

Act 1, Scene 3 – Circe the Witch

Circe's Island. It is dark. There is one sign of human habitation – a table. All is silent. Lights up on Olympus. ATHENE and POSEIDON are standing, angrily confronting each other.

POSEIDON: Odysseus has tortured my son, the Cyclops!

ATHENE: (*indignant*) But the Cyclops was going to <u>eat</u> Odysseus!

POSEIDON: Revenge is <u>mine</u>! (*Turns to look at the map.*) Where shall I send your Greek now? I know, I'll blow him south, to meet Circe the Witch. She'll finish him off in no time. Ha. Ha. Ha. (*He folds his arms smugly and turns away from her.*)

ATHENE: (*despairingly*) My wisdom won't help Odysseus when he meets Circe the Witch.

(*There is a sound of chimes. HERMES whizzes in, holding a stick.*)

HERMES: Magic will help Odysseus. (*Gestures with his Moly stick.*) Look! Holy Moly. A magic stick to fight off witchcraft.

ATHENE: Holy Moly! Go, Hermes – <u>go</u>!

(*HERMES exits to the sound of chimes. ATHENE and POSEIDON sit down on Olympus. CREW take up their boat formation and row.*)

VOICE ONE: Poseidon blew up a storm that sent the Greeks spinning to the Island of Circe the Witch!

VOICE TWO: Strange animals came out to greet them. Wild animals that sought the company of men...

(*CHORUS make wild, jungle sounds as the ANIMALS enter and start to prowl around the forest, centre stage. The CREW stand and leave their boat, intrigued by the animals.*)

MENTOR: Trojan Horses! Look at this lot.

ELPENOR: Weird! (*A lion fawns on him and miaows sadly.*) Why do they like us so much?

(*A tiger presses against Mikos and rubs her head against his knee.*)

MIKOS: Look how tame they are!

(The ANIMALS yowl and lope off forlornly.)

ODYSSEUS: *(spooked)* There's <u>something</u> sinister about this island... something unnatural.

EURYLOCHUS: *(hiding behind Polites)* Oh, no! You can't see a Cyclops, can you?

ODYSSEUS: No, but there <u>is</u> evil here. I can smell it!

EURYLOCHUS: <u>Everywhere</u> we go there's evil! Can't you smell something good for a change? Like roast lamb or spicy sausage...? I'm starving!

ELPENOR: Then go and search the island for some nuts and berries.

EURYLOCHUS: *(livid)* I'm a <u>hero</u> – not a hedgehog!

POLITES: Come on, let's have a snoop around. You never know what we might find... *(CREW exit.)*

(ODYSSEUS is left alone. On Olympus HERMES stands up and runs onto the stage where he stops before ODYSSEUS, holding his Holy Moly.)

HERMES: Face to face with the hero at last! I am Hermes, Messenger of the Gods.

ODYSSEUS: <u>Hermes</u>! *(He salutes the God.)* Divine Messenger – I salute you.

HERMES: Salute the Goddess Athene, she's the one who's looking after you. *(Hands the stick to ODYSSEUS.)* Here take this...

ODYSSEUS: A stick? Er... Thank you.

HERMES: *(impatiently)* It's <u>not</u> a stick, you mortal twit! It's Moly, magic to you. You'll need it when you meet Circe.

ODYSSEUS: The Witch – here?

HERMES:	Of course – it's <u>her</u> island! *(He heads back to Olympus.)*
ODYSSEUS:	*(calling after HERMES)* Thank you, Hermes. I'll keep your Moly close to my heart. *(Tucks the Moly into his tunic.)* Now, where are my men? Polites, Elpenor, Stavros...? *(He exits, calling their names.)*

(Enter CIRCE carrying a tray of delicious food and a wand. She places the food on the table.)

CIRCE:	*(smiling wickedly at the audience)* I am Circe, the Witch! Watch me make pigs of men. Ah, look, here come my victims now...

(The CREW enter and jump in fright at the sight of CIRCE.)

CREW:	Ahhh!
CIRCE:	*(smiling temptingly)* Welcome, strangers. Welcome to my island.

(The CREW stare past her and gaze in wonder at the food on the table.)

EURYLOCHUS:	Look at that lot!
CASTOR:	Where are we? What is the name of your kingdom?
CIRCE:	All will be revealed after you have eaten. Come, eat.

(The CREW run eagerly to the table and mime eating the food. CIRCE taps each in turn with her wand. They stop eating and fall down under the table, where they quickly put on their pig masks and emerge as pigs, on their knees, grunting.)

CREW:	Oink! Oink! Oink!

(CIRCE laughs wickedly, then stops as Odysseus enters.)

CIRCE:	Down, swine! Here comes your master. Welcome, stranger, welcome to my island.

ODYSSEUS: *(bowing)* My name is Odysseus – *(The grunting pigs barge him.)* Ow! What the heck –

CIRCE: *(shooing pigs away)* Out swine – <u>out</u>!

(Pigs scuttle nervously away from the witch.)

CIRCE: Come Odysseus, eat!

ODYSSEUS: Thank you, gracious lady. *(He mimes eating from the tray.)* Mmmmmm! This is delicious!

(CIRCE creeps up and taps ODYSSEUS with her wand.)

CIRCE: Hah! Got you!

(ODYSSEUS holds his Moly high, like a crucifix. CIRCE cringes before him.)

ODYSSEUS: No! I've got you, witch. Now tell me – <u>where are my men</u>?

(PIGS come scampering on, grunting excitedly around the table.)

CIRCE: *(mockingly)* Don't you recognise them, Odysseus?

ODYSSEUS: <u>Pigs</u>! *(He thrusts the Moly stick in her face.)* Turn them back to men or you die!

(CIRCE wastes no time in tapping the pigs with her wand.)

CIRCE: Pigs to men, now back again.

(Under the table the CREW remove their masks and reappear as men.)

CREW: <u>Witch</u>!

(CIRCE runs from the angry men.)

CIRCE: Ah! Odysseus, don't let them hurt me!

ODYSSEUS: Why should I help <u>you</u>?

CIRCE:	*(slyly)* Because I know the secrets of the Deep and I could save you an unnecessary trip to Hades.
ELPENOR:	That sounds like a good idea to me.
STAVROS:	Tell us then.
CIRCE:	First, you will meet the Sirens.
POLITES:	The Sirens? Aren't they beautiful women?
CIRCE:	You fool! They're monsters disguised as beautiful women. Listen to me, Odysseus. These Sirens will sing a song as you pass their island. A song so beautiful you will want to stop and listen – but you mustn't!
ODYSSEUS:	*(unconvinced)* Why not?
CIRCE:	*(menacingly)* Because they will eat you alive!
EURYLOCHUS:	*(wriggling uncomfortably)* Ugh! That's a good enough reason for me!
CIRCE:	Odysseus, when you sail past their island you must stuff wax in your crew's ears so that none of them will hear the song of the Sirens.
ODYSSEUS:	*(proudly)* But I must hear their song. I'm a hero!
CIRCE:	Then your crew must tie you tightly to the masthead – otherwise you'll jump overboard and swim to the Sirens... and die!
ELPENOR:	Do other evils await us?
CIRCE:	Scylla and Charybdis!
STAVROS:	Scylla, the six-headed monster!
MIKOS:	And Charybdis, the deadly whirlpool!

ODYSSEUS: How do we know you're telling the truth?

CIRCE: *(mockingly)* Oh... you'll know when you meet them. You stand no chance against Poseidon's monsters. *(Tries to detain ODYSSEUS.)* Stay here with me, my Lord? Rest...

EURYLOCHUS: *(indignant)* No way! We're not leaving him with you! He's married!

CIRCE: *(reluctantly)* Ah, farewell, Odysseus. Remember three monsters await you. The Sirens, then Scylla and Charybdis – you can't have one without the other! *(She laughs mockingly as she exits.)*

(The lights dim. All exit.)

INTERVAL

Act 2, Scene 1 – Three More Monsters

On the Sea. Lights up. We hear the sound of waves crashing. (CHORUS could do this.) The CREW sit in boat formation, peering nervously about.

CASTOR: My Lord! I can hear something. Listen...

(The CHORUS start to sing and hum hauntingly.)

STAVROS: *(terrified)* Singing!

MIKOS: The Sirens!

(The CHORUS steadily increase the volume of the song.)

CHORUS: Odysseus, come to us.
Odysseus, we love you so!
Odysseus come live with us.
Odysseus - don't go!

ELPENOR: *(mimes handing out wax)* Here, quickly, stuff wax in your ears. *(All the CREW mime stuffing wax in their ears.)*

MIKOS: *(shouting as he points to his ears)* Is that right?

EURYLOCHUS: It isn't night.

POLITES: He said right!

EURYLOCHUS: Fright? Me too, I'm terrified!

POLITES: *(bellowing)* R-i-g-h-t!

EURYLOCHUS: Don't shout at me. I've got wax in my ears!

(The SIRENS' song gets louder and more demanding. ODYSSEUS stands and listens, spellbound.)

CHORUS: O-d-y-s-s-e-u-s. Ah... Odysseus.

ODYSSEUS: I can hear them. Oh, they're so beautiful!

STAVROS: Quick, Castor! Help me tie him to the masthead.

(CASTOR and STAVROS take hold of ODYSSEUS and mime tying him to the masthead before returning to their places. ODYSSEUS stands in the middle of the boat formation with his hands behind his back.)

ODYSSEUS: Ah-h-h! I must go to them.

SIRENS: We love you, Odysseus. Ah, stay with us.
Live with us...

ODYSSEUS: *(struggling)* Set me free! Elpenor, Polites - untie me! Oh, I beg you, let me go!

ELPENOR: Row hard! Faster, faster! He's going mad!

(The CREW mime rowing hard as the CHORUS steadily increase the demanding pitch of the SIRENS' song.)

MENTOR: *(looking off stage)* Agh! Look! I can see them.
Over there – they're <u>horrible</u>!

CASTOR: *(following his gaze)* Ugh! It's an island full of rotting bones.

STAVROS: Let's get the Hades out of this place!

(As they row for their lives, ODYSSEUS continues to writhe and moan while the SIRENS bombard him with their song.)

ODYSSEUS: *(frenzied)* <u>Set me free</u>!

POLITES: <u>Row</u>! Row for your lives...

(As the CREW mime frantically rowing, the SIRENS' song decreases then fades out completely.)

CHORUS: *(in a whisper)* O-d-y-s-s-e-u-s...

ELPENOR: *(exhausted)* The Gods be praised. They've gone.

ODYSSEUS: *(slumping from the masthead)* Ah...

(The CREW crumple in the boat, their bodies heaving with exhaustion. The lights go down. Light up the CHORUS.)

VOICE ONE: The Greeks have survived the Sirens <u>but</u> ahead lie two more monsters – Scylla and Charybdis!

VOICE TWO: Just by the Straits of Messina they dwell. Scylla, a monster with <u>six</u> hideous heads. In each of her heads are three rows of rotten teeth clotted with the remains of dead men's flesh and bones!

VOICE THREE: And <u>Charybdis</u>! The deadly whirlpool who sucks sailors down into the darkness of the ocean and swallows them a-l-i-v-e!

(The lights dim over the CHORUS. Light up ATHENE on Olympus.)

ATHENE: Beware, Odysseus. <u>Beware</u>!

(Fade down Olympus. Light up the CREW, looking around nervously from their sitting positions in the boat.)

POLITES: *(from the masthead)* Look, my Lord. There are the Straits of Messina.

ODYSSEUS: Circe warned me of this place – it's Scylla's country!

EURYLOCHUS: *(weary of monsters)* Not the six-headed man-eating monster... I can't go on!

ODYSSEUS: Don't give up! We're Greek heroes – <u>row</u>! Row for your lives!

(The CREW row, chanting their war song in unison.)

CREW: We fight with Odysseus, we're his men.
                And here we are, in trouble again!
                But we'll fight and we'll fight –
                we'll <u>never</u> give up.
                Greeks don't go in for that kinda stuff!

(Light up POSEIDON, standing and speaking from Olympus.)

POSEIDON: Hah! We meet again, Greek. Here's death with six heads come to greet you. See if you can beat this!

(The six children playing SCYLLA run on, holding hands. The CHORUS combine cries and shrieks to create a menacing sound as Scylla's tentacles sneak up and curl around the CREW.)

POLITES: Ahh! Watch out!

CASTOR: Scylla's behind – ah! In front!

EURYLOCHUS: *(jumping away from the monster)* Ugh! She's all over the place!

(ODYSSEUS stands at the masthead, his sword raised.)

ODYSSEUS: You don't scare <u>me</u>, Scylla. I'll fight you like a warrior.

(He hacks at one of Scylla's heads with his sword. All the actors playing SCYLLA shriek. One grabs POLITES.)

POLITES: *(screaming in terror)* Ahhhh! She's got me.

(SCYLLA drags POLITES out of the boat formation. ODYSSEUS spins around to fight the child playing one of SCYLLA'S heads.)

ODYSSEUS: Eurylochus! Help me!

(ODYSSEUS and EURYLOCHUS push SCYLLA away as they struggle to free POLITES caught in her grip.)

EURYLOCHUS: Hah! Hah! Got you!

(POLITES falls back into the boat-formation.)

ODYSSEUS: Polites – turn the boat! Let's get out of here!

VOICE ONE: Polites turned the boat and steered a passage through Scylla's long, grasping tentacles which snatched at the men, eager for their blood and bones!

VOICE TWO: Odysseus slashed at Scylla's six screaming heads until the sea around them ran red with her blood.

CHORUS THREE: At last the hideous monster sank! Down and down she went, down into the deep to lick her wounds...

(The actors playing SCYLLA creep off stage.)

MIKOS: *(gasping for breath)* Ah... ah... the Gods be praised.

CASTOR: We survived – we beat Scylla. Yeahh!

(The lights dim. The CHORUS start to make a sinister sucking noise.)

MENTOR: *(horrified)* Oh, no!

STAVROS: Charybdis the whirlpool!

(The CHORUS in unison make a gurgling sound that rises and falls according to the action on stage. The CREW form a circle and spin around ODYSSEUS who stands in the middle of them.)

VOICES ONE
AND TWO: *(speaking over the CHORUS noises)* No sooner was Scylla gone than Charybdis the whirlpool started up his deadly sucking and blowing. The boat began to shift and break up beneath the terrified Greeks.

ODYSSEUS: *(dizzy)* Sweet Athene – <u>help me</u>!

(ATHENE stands on Olympus and blesses ODYSSEUS.)

ATHENE: Face your enemy, Odysseus. Look into the eye of the whirlpool. Look Charybdis in the <u>eye</u>!

VOICES ONE
AND TWO: *(speaking over the CHORUS noises)* Odysseus stared into the very centre of the whirlpool, commanding it with his iron will.

ODYSSEUS: *(shouting fiercely)* Suck and blow, Charybdis! You don't frighten <u>me</u>!

(The CHORUS increase their glugging sound effects. POSEIDON stands on Olympus.)

POSEIDON: *(laughing)* You're beaten this time, Odysseus. You're finished!

VOICES ONE
AND TWO: *(speaking over the CHORUS noises)* But brave Odysseus didn't give up. He stared into Charybdis's single throbbing eye...

ODYSSEUS: Back, Charybdis! <u>Back</u>!

VOICES ONE
AND TWO: Suddenly the monster dropped back into the sea.

(The CHORUS reduce their sound effects to a whisper as the CREW release each other and slip to the floor.)

ODYSSEUS: *(buckling at the knees)* Ahhh... it's gone. The Gods be praised. *(Slumps in a heap on the ground where the crew also lie exhausted.)* It's gone...

(Lights down. All exit apart from the GODS, who remain in position.)

Act 2, Scene 2 – Apollo's Sacred Bull

Apollo's Island. Lights up on Olympus where POSEIDON and ATHENE are arguing.

POSEIDON: <u>Damn him to Hades</u>! Why won't Odysseus <u>die</u>? He's had <u>everything</u>! The Cyclops, Sirens, a six-headed monster, a deadly whirlpool and he's still out there. What's wrong with him?

(HERMES springs to his feet and points towards the CREW and ODYSSEUS who are walking on stage.)

HERMES: Look! They're on the Island of the Sun God.

ATHENE: *(with dread)* Oh, no! Not Apollo's Island...?

(To the sound of loud drumbeats Zeus rises to his feet.)

ZEUS: <u>Who's</u> on the Island of Apollo the Sun God?

ATHENE: *(in a tiny, scared voice)* Odysseus.

ZEUS: <u>What</u>! Be very careful, daughter! They mustn't touch Apollo's sacred bull.

(ATHENE nods nervously.)

ZEUS: If they do – they die!

(The GODS sit and become still. Fade down Olympus. Lights up on the CREW who stand centre stage, miming chomping huge chops. ODYSSEUS in front of stage alone. ATHENE leaves Olympus. To the sound of chimes, she crosses the stage to ODYSSEUS.)

ATHENE: *(urgently)* Odysseus!

ODYSSEUS: *(falling to his knees)* Goddess! I salute you.

ATHENE: Odysseus, you are in more trouble than I ever dreamed possible.

ODYSSEUS: *(puzzled)* Trouble... but what have I done?

ATHENE: Your crew – <u>at this moment</u> – are eating Apollo's sacred bull!

ODYSSEUS: No! No!

ATHENE: I warn you, Odysseus, Zeus is on his way! Leave immediately – with or without them!

(ATHENE crosses the stage and returns to Olympus. The CREW hurry forwards, still miming eating their chops.)

EURYLOCHUS: *(wiping his mouth)* Here he is! My Lord, have we got a surprise for you.

(ODYSSEUS stands transfixed with horror.)

ODYSSEUS: No! Please tell me it's not true...

STAVROS: What a feast!

(ZEUS crosses the stage carrying his huge thunderbolt. There is the sound of loud drumbeats.)

ZEUS: <u>The bull</u>! The holy bull of the Sun God. You've eaten Apollo's bull!

ELPENOR:	Oh, help! Do something, Odysseus.
CASTOR:	*(begging)* <u>Please...</u>?
ZEUS:	It's too late. Nobody can help you now. I am Zeus, God of Gods! You must all <u>die</u>! *(ZEUS stabs the air with his thunderbolt, accompanied by thunderous drumbeats from off stage.)*

(All the CREW fall down dead. ZEUS returns to Olympus. Lights down.)

Act 2, Scene 3 – The Shadows of the Dead

In Hades. Lights up. The CREW remain in position as some of the CHORUS enter, dressed in dark cloaks – they are the DEAD. They lay a length of cloth across the stage to represent the River Styx, then slowly exit, walking like sleep walkers. The CREW slowly rise and look confused.

EURYLOCHUS:	*(spooked by the dark)* Ahhh! Where are we?
ODYSSEUS:	Idiot! We're in Hades.

(The remaining CHORUS make weird, whispering, watery noises.)

ELPENOR:	Look! There's the River Styx that separates the living from the dead.
STAVROS:	Great Balls of Fire! We <u>really</u> are in Hades.
MIKOS:	But why, Cap'n? What have we done wrong?
ODYSSEUS:	You've just eaten the Sun God's sacred bull. This is your punishment – you're dead.
EURYLOCHUS:	*(feels his arms and legs)* It's funny, I don't feel dead...
POLITES:	Ah! Look over there.

(The DEAD enter, chanting.)

ODYSSEUS: The Shadows of the Dead.

THE DEAD: Odysseus... King of Ithaca... welcome.

ODYSSEUS: Spirits from beyond. I ask to speak to Tiresias the Prophet who dwells among the Dead.

(TIRESIAS steps out from the line up of the DEAD.)

TIRESIAS: *(in an old voice)* Hail, Hero of the Greeks.

ODYSSEUS: Oh, Tiresias, wisest of men, how can I rid myself of Poseidon's vengeance?

TIRESIAS: You must never flinch from Poseidon. Never turn your back on him and never give up.

ODYSSEUS: Never give up! Look at us, the last of the mighty Greek army... *(He points to his weary CREW.)* We're exhausted!

TIRESIAS: Your men have all eternity to rest. Their journey is over.

ODYSSEUS: What! I go on alone?

TIRESIAS: Alone into the final battle.

ODYSSEUS: No! I won't leave without my friends.

(The DEAD hold out their hands to the CREW. Odysseus detains ELPENOR.)

ELPENOR: *(trying to be brave)* You must go, my Lord. We'll be all right.

THE DEAD: Come brave warriors. Cross the River Styx and enter the world of the dead...

POLITES: *(hugging Odysseus)* I shall miss you, Odysseus... pray for me.

ODYSSEUS: *(deeply moved)* I shall light a funeral pyre and build an altar in memory of all of you on my return to Ithaca.

EURYLOCHUS: This is it, Cap'n. *(Shakes hands with ODYSSEUS.)*
                     See you next time around, eh?

(The CREW step over the cloth and join the DEAD on the other side of the STYX. Slowly they walk off stage. TIRESIAS remains.)

ODYSSEUS: Goodbye my brave warriors. Goodbye...

TIRESIAS: *(commanding)* Go, Odysseus! Go home and face your final trial!

(TIRESIAS exits, leaving ODYSSEUS alone.)

ODYSSEUS: Alone... all alone. How do I get out of here...?

(Chimes sound as HERMES crosses the stage to ODYSSEUS.)

HERMES: Follow me, Odysseus – and don't look back!

(Continue 'magic' sound effects as HERMES leads ODYSSEUS off stage.)

HERMES: You're going home, Odysseus. <u>Home</u>!

(Lights dim as ODYSSEUS exits. HERMES returns to Olympus.)

Act 2, Scene 4 – The Bending of the Bow

Ithaca. Lights up. Odysseus enters and moves to centre stage where he stands looking around in dazed happiness.

ODYSSEUS: Ithaca... at last!

(A toy dog lies on the stage, it is ARGOS. Happy whining noises come from off stage.)

ARGOS: Grrr... yelp! Yelp!

ODYSSEUS: *(cuddling Argos in his arms)* Argos! Argos! Dear old friend. Twenty years since I left this very spot. Who welcomes back the hero now? Only you...

(Enter TELEMACHUS.)

TELEMACHUS: Sir! Who are you that knows my father's dog so well?

(Argos's happy whining noises turn to whimpers as he dies in his master's arms.)

ODYSSEUS: Argos...? No! *(He tenderly cradles the dog.)* His old heart is broken. Sleep, sweet friend...

TELEMACHUS: *(alarmed)* Sir! Who are you?

ODYSSEUS: His master... *(He lays Argos in the wings.)*

TELEMACHUS: *(puzzled)* Master... how?

ODYSSEUS: *(face to face with his son)* Telemachus, I am Odysseus – your father.

TELEMACHUS: Father? *(He steps back, rejecting ODYSSEUS.)* No! My father is dead.

ODYSSEUS: Nearly dead a hundred times but now I'm back, Telemachus, to tell the tale of Troy. *(He holds his arms wide open.)* My son!

TELEMACHUS: Father! It really is you! *(They embrace.)*

ODYSSEUS: *(looking around)* Where is my wife, Penelope?

TELEMACHUS: *(awkwardly)* Father, all is not well on Ithaca. While you were away, men came to claim your kingdom <u>and</u> your wife.

ODYSSEUS: They <u>what</u>?

TELEMACHUS: Have no fear. Penelope stayed faithful to you, but the suitors would not leave Ithaca.

ODYSSEUS: *(outraged)* They're <u>still</u> here – after twenty years?

TELEMACHUS: *(nodding nervously)* Y-e-s.

ODYSSEUS: *(taking Telemachus by the arm)* Come, my son – we'll
                       fight our enemies together!

*(Two SUITORS come swaggering in. TELEMACHUS pulls ODYSSEUS aside,
and whispers.)*

TELEMACHUS: The hairy one is Polybus from Crete, the other's
                       Alexander from Sparta.

(SUITORS sit centre-stage.)

ALEXANDER: Come on, be quick, get the dice rolling. *(They roll the
                       dice.)* If I win, Penelope's <u>mine</u>! Ha! Ha!

POLYBUS: You can keep the woman – I'll settle for Ithaca!

ODYSSEUS: *(livid)* How dare they talk like this! Telemachus –
                       go quickly and fetch my bow.

TELEMACHUS: Your bow?

ODYSSEUS: *(pushing him into the wings)* Ask Penelope, she'll know.

*(The SUITORS continue their game. ODYSSEUS steps forward and watches.
PENELOPE enters, with the bow. She is followed by TELEMACHUS.)*

PENELOPE: *(stopping dead when she sees ODYSSEUS)* Stranger!
                       Welcome to Odysseus's kingdom.

POLYBUS: Odysseus is dead. Marry me, Penelope.

ALEXANDER: No, me! I'm better looking.

PENELOPE: Great warriors, I am spoilt for choice. Which of you
                       to marry...?

POLYBUS: *(stunned)* You mean, after all these years, you've
                       finally chosen one of us?

PENELOPE: Yes, I've decided to marry the strongest of you.

SUITORS: *(leaping to their feet)* Me! Me!

PENELOPE: The one who can string this bow will be the next King
                    of Ithaca.

(SUITORS fight for the bow.)

PENELOPE: Wait, wait! One at a time.

TELEMACHUS: Me first.

POLYBUS: You! You're her son.

TELEMACHUS: *(taking the bow)* If I get to bend it then I rule the
                    kingdom... *(He tries his hardest to bend the bow
                    and fails.)*

ALEXANDER: Wimp! You couldn't pick a grape. *(He snatches the bow
                    from TELEMACHUS.)* Give it here! *(He tries but also
                    fails.)* Ah!

POLYBUS: *(with confidence)* Ha! Ha! That leaves me. Watch this...
                    all it needs is a <u>real man</u>! *(Falls over with the effort of
                    trying so hard.)*

ALEXANDER: Not as easy as it looks, eh?

(SUITORS scramble for another go.)

POLYBUS: Give it here!

ALEXANDER: No, get off. Let me!

ODYSSEUS: *(stepping forwards)* May I try?

(SUITORS stare at him and laugh.)

POLYBUS: <u>You</u>!

ALEXANDER: Don't make me laugh!

(ODYSSEUS takes the bow and strings it. Magic music accompanies his actions.)

POLYBUS: I don't believe it!

ALEXANDER: Who is he...?

PENELOPE: <u>Odysseus</u>! My Lord – come home!

ALEXANDER: Odysseus – you can't be serious?

POLYBUS: *(backing away)* Let's get the Hades out of here!

TELEMACHUS: *(blocking their flight path)* Why the rush? Come and meet my father! Leader of the Greeks – King of Ithaca!

POLYBUS: *(petrified)* No, please, Odysseus...

ALEXANDER: *(grovelling)* We never meant any harm...

(They run offstage, chased by ODYSSEUS aiming the bow at them.)

SUITORS: *(from off stage)* Aaaaaggghhhhh!

(ODYSSEUS walks back on stage, smiling triumphantly as he opens his arms wide.)

ODYSSEUS: Penelope!

PENELOPE: It is <u>you</u>! *(Running into his arms.)* My husband, my Lord! Ah... <u>Odysseus</u>!

ODYSSEUS: I'm h-o-m-e!

THE END

Staging

Area for Performance

I've seen this play performed in theatres, gardens, church halls and front rooms, so don't think you need the Royal Albert Hall and a cast of thousands! *The Odyssey* can be staged to suit your needs, whether it's on stage or in an acting area with rostra blocks in the school hall, or in a clear, open space at the end of your classroom.

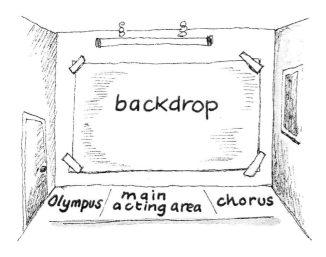

If you have a fixed stage and rostra blocks you could use the blocks to build out the stage area, to allow more space for Mount Olympus and the Greek Chorus. If you are working without stage or blocks, then simply mark off the acting area with masking tape on the floor. The main action takes place in the central area. On the left is Olympus where the Gods sit throughout the duration of the play. The Greek Chorus are positioned to the right. You might choose to give a suggestion of height to Olympus by creating a raised area of rostra blocks from which the Gods could step down when they participate in the action.

Olympus

The Gods' scenes open and close most of the longer scenes. In order to avoid umpteen noisy entrances and exits, I suggest the four actors playing the Gods remain permanently in place on Olympus. From there they can stand and speak, or rise and cross to the main stage. They'll be on stage throughout the duration of the entire play so they'll have to learn to "freeze" when they're not in action.

Backdrop

It isn't necessary to have a backdrop but many of the children would probably enjoy making one. Don't attempt to make a different backdrop for each scene; a single, all-purpose backdrop is much more practical. Once you have established how large your backdrop needs to be, use masking tape to stick together several large pieces of paper until you achieve the correct dimensions. You might choose to decorate it with a simple map of Ancient Greece.

Alternatively, you may prefer to show a typical mediterranean landscape with blue sea, sky and a Greek temple. Sketch out your map or scene in pencil before completing it with paint or collage.

Scenery and Props

There are seven scenes in *The Odyssey* which take place in seven different locations, on land, on sea, on four different islands and in Hades. Some require one or two pieces of scenery and some don't require anything as the actors themselves clarify their location.

On Land

No special scenery is required at all. However it is important to separate the land from the sea visually. This is done by the Crew forming the boat, which they do many times. It is essential that each character takes the same place <u>every</u> time, with Odysseus at the boat head and Polites, the sea captain, beside him.

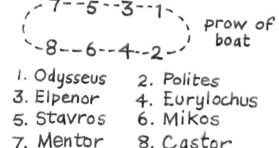

1. Odysseus
2. Polites
3. Elpenor
4. Eurylochus
5. Stavros
6. Mikos
7. Mentor
8. Castor

The Cyclops Island

No special scenery is required. The actors begin the scene by walking on stage from the front and looking around. When they find the Cyclop's cave they enter it from the back of the stage, by walking around and behind the Chorus on their right and re-entering the stage from stage left. Depending on your staging area, you may wish to construct a cave mouth and a boulder to cover it. Two coatstands covered with brown or green crepe paper could be the sides of the entrance.

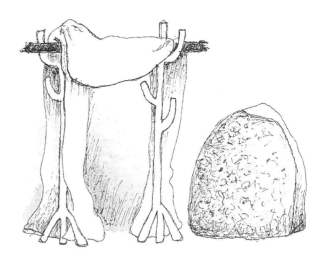

Drape these with sacks or material across the top to complete the entrance. I suggest you cut out and paint a huge cardboard boulder which the actor playing the Cyclops slams over the cave entrance. If you do not have the resources to construct the scenery, simply instruct the child playing the Cyclops to mime placing a boulder over the entrance.

Circe's Island

You will need a table in this scene, which must be big enough for the crew to hide underneath. It can be covered with a cloth, to allow the pig masks to be concealed, ready for the transformation scene.

Scenery and Props

On the Sea

The boat is created by the crew who always sit in the same positions. This helps the audience familiarise themselves with the characters and ensures there is no confusion on the crew's part when it comes to forming the boat. When Odysseus is tied to the mast head Polites and Elpenor are in the prow of the boat. Odysseus stands, miming that his hands are tied behind him, with the rest of the crew in their usual positions.

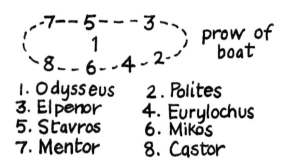

1. Odysseus
2. Polites
3. Elpenor
4. Eurylochus
5. Stavros
6. Mikos
7. Mentor
8. Castor

The six children playing Scylla in this scene run on, holding hands. They circle the boat and writhe their bodies in union as they press themselves upon the crew. The Chorus combine whispers and cries to create a weird, menacing sound as Scylla's tentacles (ie. the children's hands) twist and turn around the terrified crew.

To create the Charybdis whirlpool effect the crew wrap their arms firmly around each other and start to spin as the Chorus combine to make the sucking, gurgling sounds of the whirlpool. As the sound effects increase and reach fever pitch the crew spin faster and faster <u>and</u> faster! It will take a fair amount of practice to get this routine co-ordinated but it can look very convincing, especially with lighting.

In Hades

To make the River Styx, take a length of silky blue cloth. Lining material is cheap, vivid and very effective. Two of the Dead lay it widthways across the stage, to mark the line between the living and the dead. For extra effectiveness the stage management team could hold the ends in the wings and gently ripple the cloth as the Crew step over.

Scenery and Props

Small Props

I've tried to keep the props to a minimum as I know, from the most bitter experience, that too many props in a children's play is a recipe for disaster! A lot of the props are mimed in the playscript but you might like to mime even more. I've marked some possibles with an asterisk. It's a good idea to set up a props table from which the actors collect their own props.

A rough bowl and some cheese*
(Act 1, Scene 2)
Odysseus' bottle of Nectar
(Act 1, Scene 2)
A red-hot stick*
(Act 1, Scene 2)
Eight sheep fleeces or pieces of white
    sheeting*
(Act 1, Scene 2)
Circe's banquet on a tray
Pig masks
(Act 1, Scene 3)
Cardboard beef bones
(Act 2, Scene 2)
Argos, the toy dog
(Act 2, Scene 4)
Odysseus' bow
(Act 2, Scene 4)

Odysseus' bottle of Nectar
This can be made by attaching a length of thick twine to a smallish green plastic fizzy drink bottle so the actor can carry it over his shoulder.

The Cyclop's Stick
Use an old broom handle and paint the end to create the red-hot tip.

Sheep Fleeces
If you can lay your hands on half a dozen real fleeces, they would be perfect. Alternatively, use a thick marker pen to draw a sheep outlines on old sheeting and cut these out. They need to cover the crew's head, and shoulders.

A tray of sumptuous food
To make Circe's banquet stick plastic or papier mâché food and fruit onto a tray.

Argos
You will need a large floppy toy dog for Argos — one that will look dead when it needs too! If you use a soft toy, Odysseus can make the head droop pathetically as he cradles the dying dog in his arms.

The bow
This is used in the play's triumphant finale so it has to be effective but safe. If you can borrow a real bow that would be excellent. Otherwise take a plastic hoop, one that you might use for P.E., cut it in half and string it with golden ribbon.

Lighting

This play is particularly impressive if you have, or can hire, theatrical lighting. It creates a real atmosphere, especially in the monster scenes, and also helps to differentiate between the land and the sea scenes. There are some lighting directions in the playscript.

If you have no special lighting at all, don't worry! You can draw blinds or curtains to cut out the daylight, or create an atmosphere by turning the hall lights off before the audience arrives, then turn them on just before the play starts, to let them know something is about to happen. Turn them off at the interval and back on again for Act 2. Make sure the Chorus and Olympus are clearly lit and that the musicians and sound effects team have enough light to see by.

Casting and Auditions

Who's who...?

My heart always goes out to the desperately keen children who long for a star part yet always finish up playing the donkey! Explain right at the start of the auditions that there's a part for everybody.

Because *The Odyssey* is apparently a predominantly male cast the boys may try to lay claim to it. Stress that it's a mixed cast or you might lose the girls' interest.

The children who have an eye on the big parts must understand that there'll be a lot of lines to memorize and that you will expect them to learn their parts and not let the rest of the cast down. The Greek Chorus is a perfect way in for all those shy children who might be hiding their light under a bushel. If you take into consideration all the lines spoken by the Chorus both as a group and as individual "voices", there should be some sort of speaking part for everyone who wants it.

For those children who wish to remain out of the limelight, explain that you'll be looking for dancers, musicians and a stage management team. Make sure the children understand that these parts are just as crucial to the production as the main speaking roles and are not necessarily an easy option!

Casting and Auditions

The Auditions

Before you begin, I suggest you talk to the children about the story of the play and explain the background. Explain who the main characters are, using the descriptions on pages 42–43 to help you. Then they will have some idea of the play before you begin the group audition.

Auditions can be a lot of fun but you do get the inevitable situation where the confident ones shine and the quieter ones withdraw. A sneaky way round this problem is to take some gripping scenes from *The Odyssey* and turn them into P.E. games. Here are two examples.

* As most of the scenes end with Odysseus and the Crew jumping into their boat and rowing for their lives, why not start with the boat formation? Divide the class into groups of eight. Give them the names of all the crew, explaining that Odysseus is the leader and Polites is the sea captain, then let them choose their character. Once they've settled down in the specified boat formation, start up a slow beat on a drum or with woodblocks. Tell the children to row in unison. When they're familiar with the regular rhythm, increase the beat to a faster, more frantic rhythm. End the exercise with a slow beat as the boat drifts in on the incoming tide.

* Add Scylla to the boat sequence. Juggle the numbers as necessary, two sets of six for the dancers, two sets of eight for the boat. As the crew row, the dancers playing Scylla surround them. They make weird, eerie noises as they writhe and press themselves against the boat, trying to drag the crew down into the sea with their long, snakey tentacles! Watch carefully how each of the crew members react.

Now try the following drama exercises:

* Divide the children into groups of nine to act out Act 1, Scene 2 from the point at which Odysseus gives the Cyclops a drink through to the end of the scene.

* Divide the children into groups of nine to act out part of Act 1, Scene 3, from Circe's entrance to the moment when the crew are turned back from pigs into men.

* Divide the children into groups of four to improvise the conversation in Act 1, Scene 1 between Poseidon, Hermes, Zeus and Athene.

Be sure that the children playing the Gods <u>really</u> can sit still. Try Sleeping Gods as a variation on the game Sleeping Logs, it's a sure fire way of spotting the twitchers!

The Main Characters

Odysseus
Brave, clever and much loved by
his men.

Elpenor
Odysseus' best friend. The leader
in Odysseus' absence.

Circe
A clever, cruel and very
sneaky witch!

Polyphemus the Cyclops
Poseidon's son. A huge, one-eyed monster, who loves
eating strangers for supper.

Eurylochus
Noisy, funny and always
hungry!

Polites
The sea captain. He takes control on the
stormy seas.

Poseidon
The Sea God with a
heck of a temper. Zeus'
brother.

Zeus
Father of the Gods.
All powerful.

Athene
Beautiful Goddess of
Wisdom. Zeus'
favourite daughter.

Telemachus
Odysseus' son.

Hermes
Messenger of the Gods.

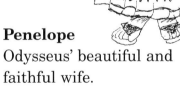

Penelope
Odysseus' beautiful and
faithful wife.

The Stage Management Team

A reliable stage management team is essential to any good production, the very backbone of the show. They will need to attend rehearsals from the start.

Director's Assistant
Your right-hand girl or boy who makes lists, takes messages and reminds you of everything you've forgotten to do!

Lighting
If you have theatrical lighting an adult must supervise. One assistant may be needed. If you're using ceiling lighting, a child can do this, as long as you've gone through the lighting cues in the playscript.

Props Table
It's wise to have one person solely responsible for this job. They should have a list of the small props (see page 39) and check that they're on the props table for the actors to collect before the beginning of each act.

Scene Shifters
Although there is little movement of scenery in the play, two people will certainly be needed for this job.

Prompter
You'll need a good reader for this very important role. Position the prompter offstage, with their own copy of the script, ready to remind the actors of their lines.

Sound Effects Team
Particularly vital in this play where there are so many sound effects. They should have their own copy of the play with their own individual cues highlighted, plus the instruments or items required to make the sound effects (see page 48).

Front of House
Two smiling children to welcome the audience, show them to their seats and give out programmes, which of course the class will have designed themselves!

Rehearsal Schedule

The children will need to know exactly when the serious rehearsals begin. Check out with the rest of the staff how much time you can set aside during school hours and contact the parents to find out how much time is available to the childen after school hours. Once this is established, draw up a rehearsal list which nobody is expected to deviate from – not even for a visit to the dentist!

Be sure to give yourself a longer rehearsal time for the Technical Run, when the stage management team co-ordinate their individual roles. In my experience it's always fraught, exhausting and goes way over time so it's best to alert the parents that their children might be late that day. The same applies to the Final Dress Rehearsal, when make-up, hair and costumes are all assembled for the first time and nearly everything goes wrong!

Costume

This is the bit we all love and the moment when the real magic starts. As they transform themselves into their characters, the children suddenly seem to realise the immensity of what they're about to do. It's at this point you have to keep a tight grip on the primadonnas in your midst!

Male Roles

The basic costume for many of the male parts will be a tunic, worn with a belt. The tunics can easily be made from two rectangles of cloth, which should be sewn across the shoulders and up the sides. The different roles will be distinguished by length, colour and decoration.

The Crew
They will all wear short tunics in dull colours such as brown or grey. You may choose to distinguish Polites and Elpenor by giving their costumes a decorative border in a dark colour such as black. The crew will all need pig masks for Act 1, Scene 3 (see page 47).

Odysseus
To differentiate Odysseus from his men and to remind the audience that he is a King, paint his Greek border in gold. Odysseus also carries a sword. It would be fine to use a plastic toy sword but it is also possible to make one from stiff cardboard and paint it silver if you prefer.

The Gods
It is important to distinguish Gods from mortals through their costume. The decorative borders on their tunics should be done in silver or gold. They should all wear golden laurel wreaths on their heads. For each wreath you need a 1m length of picture wire. Draw your leaves on plain stiff card and cut them out. For each child you will probably need about 15–20 leaves. Spray the leaves gold, thread them onto the wire and twist the wreath around the child's head.

Zeus needs to look very dignified. He should wear a long yellow or gold tunic, with a golden sash. He will carry a thunderbolt which can be cut from a large piece of stiff card. This will also need to be painted silver or gold.

Costume

Poseidon can be dressed in a long, flowing blue-green tunic, with a sash and a trident. Cut the trident from a piece of stiff card and paint it silver or gold. **Hermes** will wear a short white tunic with a gold sash belt and a gold stick, rather like a twiggy wand.

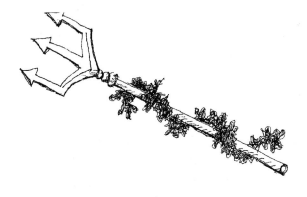

The Cyclops

Try to pick the tallest child in the class for this part and create further height and terror-impact by adding an enormous monster head. Take a tall cardboard box and paint it brown. Cut a big circle out of it, for the monster's single eye. Glue a clump of old fur or a tangle of black and brown wool on top of the box, for the monster's tangled hair. The Cyclops should wear brown leggings and a matching brown top with long sleeves.

Tiresias

This character must look as old as time. Paint his face a pasty white to contrast with his full-length, hooded grey tunic. Make the tunic as usual and attach a hood made from two pieces of material, sewn together as shown.

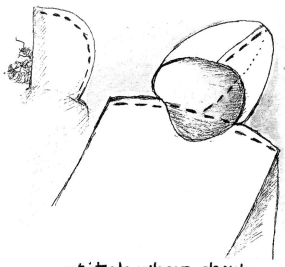

----stitch where shown

Telemachus

He can wear a short tunic decorated with gold motif.

Female Roles

Athene

As a goddess, she will need a gold laurel wreath. She will wear a long, white tunic trimmed with silver. She should carry a spear which could be made from bamboo cane, sprayed in silver and topped with a blade of silver foil or card.

Costume

Circe

She should wear a red dress or tunic, with a circlet of red paper poppies in her hair. The circlet can be made in a similar way to the laurel wreaths. Cut the poppies out of stiff red card and thread them onto a length of picture wire.

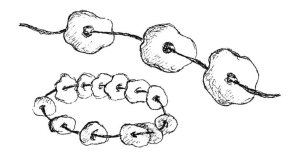

Penelope

She is a Queen, so add a royal gold motif to the hem of her long dress and a golden crown, which can be quite simply made from a piece of card sprayed with gold.

Unisex Roles

Scylla

The six children playing Scylla require black leotards and black leggings. They'll all need identical masks to represent the monster's six ugly heads. They can paint these themselves — don't forget the fangs! Use fine elastic to secure the masks.

string on picture or garden wire

The Chorus

The Chorus should all wear long, white shifts, based on the tunic design on page 45.

The Dead

The Dead wear ragged dark tunics, similar to Tiresias' costume. These must be hooded so that they can be drawn over the actors' faces, adding an even spookier effect!

The Animals

They'll need leggings and leotards or tee shirts and masks. The children playing the animals might like to make their own masks using this basic template to which they'll have to add their animal's characteristic features. The mask should sit on the top of the head, rather than cover the child's face. Attach elastic to go under the chin and pipe cleaner whiskers.

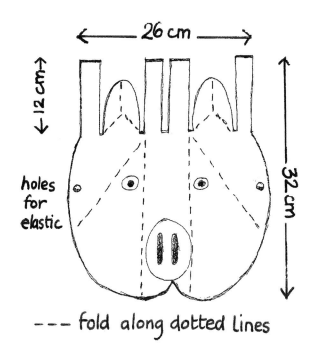

26 cm

12 cm

holes for elastic

32 cm

--- fold along dotted lines

Music

The Crew's war song (in Act 1, Scene 1 and Act 2, Scene 1) is a loud, boisterous chant. For greater gusto add loud drum beats. The Song of the Sirens, sung by the Chorus, rises and falls hauntingly. It could be set to the same tune as "My Bonny lies over the Ocean" but a keen musical member of staff might come up with something more alluring and hypnotic!

Magic music for the Bending of the Bow in the final scene can be made with a combination of tinkling triangles and a chime bar.

Sound Effects

This play really does benefit from the sound effects written into the playscript. Fortunately the Chorus provide the most complicated effects but there are quite a few more needed. Here's a list to refer to:

The Chorus Sound Effects

Poseidon's storm
(Act 1, Scene 1)
The Cyclops' sheep
(Act 1, Scene 2)
The jungle noises of Circe's wild animals
(Act 1, Scene 3)
The menacing hiss and shriek of Scylla
(Act 2, Scene 1)
The sucking and gurgling of Charybdis
(Act 2, Scene 1)
A weird, whispering water noise in
Hades
(Act 2, Scene 3)

Further Sound Effects

Clashing cymbals
Wind chimes or triangles for the Gods' entrances and exits
Wood blocks for the rhythm of the Crew's rowing
Very loud drum beats
Happy dog whines followed by sad whimpers. The effects person will need to practise co-ordinating these sounds with the actions on stage!
The pre-recorded sound of crashing waves.

Final Word

Keep calm, especially during the final tech run and the dress rehearsal when you will seriously wonder why you ever bothered! Believe me it will be worth all your hard work when you see the children playing their parts on stage and afterwards you'll all be inundated with praise!